Book Three of the
Broden and Cookie Series

D1403417

Broden Wants To Quit

Written and Illustrated by Katie Coughran

For inquiries, email katiecoughranbooks@gmail.com

ISBN-13: 978-1539821298

ISBN-10: 1539821293

For every kid that ever wanted to quit piano

CONTENTS

1 NO, NO, NO!

"SING IT WHILE YOU play it—the way your piano teacher taught you, Broden," his mother called from the kitchen and Broden thought that he'd rather eat a slug sandwich with cockroaches on the side.

In fact, there were about a million things that he didn't like *at all* that he would rather be doing than playing the *piano.*

He'd prefer scooping up chicken dung, doing homework, or being shoved by Fergus the school bully. He'd even choose having gum stuck on the bottom of his incredible skate shoes, being chased through the yard by Tim the Terrible Squirrel, or being forced to take a nap.

Maybe I'll try that, Broden thought, hopped off the bench and hurried to the kitchen with the idea that might get him out of playing those horrible keys.

Just in time, he caught himself rushing and slowed down, dragging his feet and faking a yawn to convince his mother.

"Oh, Mom. I don't think I can practice right now—I'm so *tired*. I think I need to take a little nap," Broden said, rubbing his eyes with his fist. Then he faked one more ginormous yawn for good measure.

"Really . . .that tired, huh?" Mom said lovingly and came over to give him a hug.

Broden snuggled back, hoping that it would get him out of practicing and thought, *Yes . . .yes! It's working!*

Still in his mother's embrace, she said softly, "Broden, I'm going to tell you something."

"Mhmm?"

"I saw you running in just before faking weariness, you stinker!" she said laughing, turning the hug into a tickle that he squirmed away from. "Get to practicing and *then* you can take a nap."

Broden walked away from the kitchen, letting his head fall forward, shaking it in despair. "No. No! No, no, no. No more practicing! I don't want to!"

"Son, go and practice. *Right. Now.*"

Broden looked at his mother, saw her cocked eyebrow, hand on hip and knew that he wasn't winning this one.

Slumping off to the piano bench, Broden dragged himself back onto it, thinking, *How did I get into this mess? How did I get talked into taking lessons?*

Pouting on the bench, his thoughts kept his hands from moving to the keys and after several minutes passed, his mother came in carrying something. It was Eagle Man; Hero of the World.

"Put this away when you're done practicing, please," Mrs. Tunney said putting his action figure down, then looked at him sternly. "And get going. *You* are the one that wanted to learn to play the piano. *You* made the commitment, son. Now you need to keep it."

Broden wished his mother wasn't right, but she was. He *had* begged to learn and he *had* made the commitment.

The only problem was that he hadn't realized that he would need to practice in order to learn. And he hadn't known exactly how much he wouldn't like practicing.

Broden wasn't sure that, being only nine years old, he had really known exactly what sort of trouble he was getting himself into. It was a pretty *big* commitment for a kid.

And on second thought, maybe he *hadn't* begged. Maybe he hadn't even *asked* to play the piano. *Why would I do that?*

Maybe his mother just wanted him to, and he had been tricked into taking the music lessons.

"Mommy!" his little seven-year-old sister, Ellie, yelled from upstairs.

His mother walked away with a pointed finger and said, "Practice *now*, Broden Tunney."

"Yes, Mom," he grumbled, then played a chord in the left hand while he started plunking out the notes to the song he had been singing for a long, long

time before any piano teacher had assigned it—the song he guessed he'd have to keep on singing forever. "A...B...C...D..."

Finally hearing his mother close the door of Ellie's room right when he sang the letter 'R', Broden bent over and snatched up Eagle Man.

As Broden moved Eagle Man's big arm forward while tucking both of his wings backward, Broden got the action figure positioned so that the winged, muscular man with taloned feet was ready to help him.

"Alright, Eagle Man. Let's play," Broden said, and began using Eagle Man's outstretched arm to clink out the rest of the alphabet. "S...T...U...V..."

He played the last few notes and then Broden let out a groan and threw his head back as soon as he was done with his...performance. "Eagle Man, Mom said I have to play it three more times, but..."

As Broden thought about how to get out of practicing, he started goofing off and clinking around with Eagle Man's arm. And his wings. And his taloned feet. "Hey! That sounds just like your theme song, Eagle man!"

With that, the alphabet left his head, and he and Eagle Man got to work on playing and singing the theme song from his very favorite cartoon.

"Eagle Man Soar! Eagle Man Fly! Eagle Man will see you with his awesome eye! Bad guys, run away as fast as you can—if you don't you'll get caught by an eagle that's half man—" Broden sang until he was unexpectedly interrupted.

"Broden Tunney, what on *earth* are you *doing?*" Mrs. Tunney cried, cutting off Eagle Man's theme song that Broden was playing all wrong. "I have asked you and asked you. And yet, you're still not practicing!"

Broden sighed, feeling guilty, and his hands dropped down with Eagle Man.

Of course, he'd forgotten the booming sound that it would make when his palms and the plastic figure came *terwanging* and pounding down onto the keys.

At the incredibly loud sound, his mother looked at him like she'd just eaten the sourest of candies, startling Broden so much that he dropped Eagle Man.

Then things got *worse*. She said, "Broden, when your father gets home, you'll be speaking with *him*. Now. *Go to your room until he gets here.*"

"But, Mom—" Broden began, but his mother interrupted.

"If you don't get upstairs, *I'll* be doing ollies on your skateboard instead of *you*. For a *week*."

Broden turned and ran as if a T-rex were chasing him, snapping at his heals.

He did *not* want to lose his skateboard for *seven whole days*.

Flinging his door open, he charged inside, throwing the door closed behind him. Scowling, he looked around for something to do and was upset when he realized that he'd left Eagle Man downstairs.

"Ugh!" Broden grunted, then grabbed an Eagle Man: Hero of the World comic book he had just picked up from the library. He read it once, then again. Then he grabbed something else to read.

The problem was, he was getting bored. *Really* bored. Looking at his watch, he checked the time and then sighed again before mumbling, "This is worse than practicing."

It seemed like a bazillion, katrillion years before he heard his father's truck pull into the driveway. Jumping up from the bed, he yanked on the string that drew up the blinds and looked down into the yard.

As soon as his father opened up the truck, he heard his mother close the front door and saw her appear next to the truck, her hands on her hips.

Broden couldn't hear what they said, but he saw their faces when they were talking. Mrs. Tunney looked angry and Mr. Tunney looked like he was preparing for battle.

But then something very interesting

happened. They spoke for some time before coming inside and Broden thought it was very strange. When they were walking into the house, his mother looked triumphant, but his father looked…well, like he usually did when he came home from work. Pleasant, relaxed and ready to be home.

Huh, Broden thought to himself, then ran downstairs when he heard his mother calling.

2 THE SCARIEST
SOUND IN THE WORLD

MR. AND MRS. TUNNEY sat in the kitchen at the table across from Broden. He gulped when he looked at his mother, then relaxed a little when he looked at his father. It was all very confusing.

"Broden, your mother says that you haven't been practicing the piano today," his father said, *kind of* sternly. And was it his imagination, or was there a little twinkle in his eye?

"Broden hasn't been practicing for

weeks," his mother snapped, eyebrows furrowed. "He just sits down and goofs around. Or he'll play *much* too quickly and not the way his teacher says. And *today* I found him playing on the keys with a *toy!*"

"Why aren't you practicing the way you're supposed to, son? And why are you ruining the piano with your toys?" Mr. Tunney asked, a stern look appearing as the twinkle disappeared a little.

"I wasn't *trying* to ruin the piano, Broden mumbled. "I don't like it, dad. It's really hard, I don't like any of the songs—they're for *babies*—and practicing is the *worst.*"

"You *have* to start with the basics,

16

Broden! You can play Mr. Eagle—"Eagle Man, Mom!" Broden interrupted—or whatever else you want to play later on. But right *now*, learn the simple things," Mrs. Tunney said, cocking her eyebrow when Broden interrupted her with his correction.

"Anna, please," Mr. Tunney said gently, but Mrs. Tunney didn't like it one bit. Now she cocked her eyebrow at *him*. "Well, Anna, we should *listen* to him."

"Liam, I *have* been listening to him. Listening to him complain. Listening to him *not practice*. I've been patient and I've been as helpful as I can. But he *just won't practice*." Mrs. Tunney let out a massive huff, stood up and stuck her hands on

her hips and glared.

"Maybe this just isn't worth it, then, Anna. These lessons are expensive, the boy won't practice and he says he doesn't even *like* it," Mr. Tunney said and Broden couldn't believe his ears. Was his father actually going to take his side?

Broden couldn't really remember his parents ever fighting before. Sometimes he heard them talking seriously in their room, but this seemed different. They were arguing *right in front of him*. About his stinky, old piano lessons!

Not that he *wanted* his parents to argue, but if they were going to, he wanted it to be about piano lessons. Wouldn't that mean that he might have a chance of getting out of the scariest trap in the world?

"He *would* like it—if he would *practice*, Liam. But he won't do it the right way without me sitting right next to him. Broden's too big for that—he ought to do it on his own," his mother said with finality.

"How can you expect a little boy to sit down and *practice* by himself every day? I just don't think it's reasonable. I don't think he's ready for this and I think it's a waste of time and money," his father said, sitting back in his chair with his arms folded across his chest. "I think we should let him quit."

Although Broden was insulted that his

father had called him a little boy, it was at that moment when Broden smiled.

Inside his mind, fireworks were going off at the thought of being able to quit. *Kaboom! Kaboom! I get to Quit!*

Broden felt so light and happy at the thought that he felt like he might just float off of the ground like a balloon. He would rather quit than have all of the candy in the *whole world*.

"Liam," his mother said quietly—the scariest sound Broden had *ever* heard. It gave him worse chills than Criss-Cross-Applesauce. It was *frightening*. "Our son made a commitment. And Broden quitting is *not* what we agreed to, Liam Tunney."

Broden's mouth dropped open—she only used full names for Ellie and him!

Silently, he watched as his mother turned from the table, opened the back door with the window in it and slammed it harder than a giant would be able to.

It seemed as if the whole house shook, and it rattled Broden's smile right off of his face.

Looking at his father, Broden saw that he didn't feel pleasant, relaxed or ready to be home anymore. He looked upset and Broden could see that he was thinking very hard.

Awkwardly sitting across from his father, he wondered if he could get up, but Broden didn't think that was quite the right thing to do.

Still as could be, his father sat for a long time.

A *very* long time.

"Son," Mr. Tunney said finally and looked up at Broden. "You get to the piano and practice. And I never want to hear that you have done a poor job of it again. Understand?"

Broden gulped, then nodded and went to the piano. The sick feeling in his stomach told him that his parent's decision was final, and that arguing would get him into deep trouble.

And he guessed that his dad was scared of Mom, too.

3 PRACTICING FOR REAL

THE NEXT DAY WHEN Broden got into the van after school, his mother handed him an apple and smiled at him.

"Broden, eat this up, then you get fifteen minutes to do whatever you want when we get home. After that, it's time to practice," Mrs. Tunney said.

Broden let out a groan, but she whipped her head around and gave him the evil eye.

Ahh! Broden thought, looking at her crazy-squid-eyes-about-to-eat-you face, then he quickly stopped groaning.

"And I'm going to help you practice, Broden. Your father was right about that. It's difficult to learn something new without any help." Mrs. Tunney smiled at him, but he couldn't decide if it looked more like a crocodile's smile than his mother's smile.

"Ok, Mom," he said uncertainly, hoping her crocodile mouth didn't snap, then quietly ate the apple she'd brought for him.

They soon drove down the dirt road to the Tunney house and Broden immediately got out his skateboard. Hurrying, he pulled out his small collection of trick equipment he'd gathered—cones and the ramp and grind rail he and his father had built.

Pushing off with his foot, he began skating across his driveway, up the ramp, through the cones, and attempting to slide his board across the grind rail.

"*Buk, buk, buk-a-buk-a-buk-buk,*" came the sound of his favorite pet.

"Hiya Cookie!" Broden said and skated over to the little black hen. He couldn't believe that he hadn't wanted her when they first moved to the country. "How's your day been?"

Cookie furrowed her brow and looked super angry. Then she let out a little growl and showed off her shark teeth before jumping up and flapping up to his shoulder, angrily adjusting her feathers.

Broden skated around with the chicken perched on his shoulder like a parrot while she told him all kinds of stories that he thought must be about the other chickens and maybe even Tim the Terrible. Cookie and Tim, the squirrel, often had troubles.

"Buk, buk, buk-a-buk-a-BOK BOK BOOOOOOK!!!!" she ended furiously.

"It's ok, Cookie," Broden said, patting her back. "Don't forget that the reason Tim has a chunk of his tail missing is because of *you*."

But this didn't seem to comfort her. She just cocked her head at Broden, rolled her eye at him, then went on muttering *buk buks.*

"I have troubles of my own," Broden said when his mother opened the door.

"Time to practice, Broden," she called, then closed the door behind her.

"No…no, no, no," he muttered, realizing he sounded a *lot* like Cookie.

Patting Cookie once more, he said, "I have to go in, now. I'll be back in a bit."

Cookie flapped away and he shuffled his feet into the house. Then he washed his hands—not because he really cared if his hands had glue and marker and gum and some leftover crackers stuck in the glue and gum. And now a tiny chicken feather, too. But because it made it take longer to get to the piano. So he washed

his hands. *Really well.*

"Those hands look perfectly clean for practicing. Let's go," Mrs. Tunney said, not falling for his trick when she appeared in the bathroom doorway.

For the next thirty minutes, Broden tried super-duper, extra hard to be good. He *tried,* even though he didn't think that he could bear to play one more note, or count any more beats.

"1, 2, 3, 4, 1, 2, 3, 4," his mother said while he sang the alphabet. *Again.*

"Check your fingers," his mother said and he moved his ring finger to the proper note.

"Oooh! Fix that note, Broden," she said patiently, and Broden thought that he might start crying.

"Ok, one last time! Then you're done, Broden," his mother said and he thought that his head might pop like a balloon. There was *no way* he could play it *again*.

"Mom, I…" he began to complain, but then he remembered the night before.

It was bad enough to have a crocodile smile practicing with him, but he didn't want his father to turn into a wolf when he came home from work and found out that he'd been naughty during practice. Quickly, he changed his words to say, "I'm ready."

"1, 2, 3, 4…A, B, C, D…fix your notes…check your fingering…count evenly…last note and you're done!" his mother said and his finger pushed down the last key to finish the piece. "Good job!"

"Thanks," Broden croaked. Letting out a deep sigh, he felt like he'd been rolled down a bumpy hill, *womp, womp, womp* all the way down.

Looking at his mother, Broden waited for her to say the magic words that excused from the piano.

"You may go and play. Good work," his mother said and the crocodile seemed to be gone. Only the gentle, lovely smile of his mother remained.

Broden jumped up from the bench and ran like a ghost was after him until he made it outside. He didn't want his mother to change her mind and tell him to try just *one more time*. She had said 'one more time' *four* times on the last piece.

"Cookie!" Broden called as he grabbed his skateboard. She came around the corner, her head bobbing front and back as she walked over.

Rolling the board toward her, Cookie spread her wings out and *ran* over to it.

Hopping on, she flapped hard to pick up speed, then popped the skateboard up on the grind rail. She slid across perfectly, landing it, *quonk,* on the other side.

"Yeah, Cookie!" Broden said and ran to put the chicken on his shoulder, Cookie smiling her toothy smile at him.

Kicking off, Broden began skating

around with his little hen perched like a parrot. He was glad that he was done practicing that stinky old piano for the day.

4 FERGUS FINDS OUT

On Thursday, Broden got into the van with his piano books in his backpack when they headed to school.

Though he thought it was torture, he had practiced solidly for five days with his mother helping him and he could zoom through his pieces now.

The problem was, he cared more about socks full of toe-jam than he cared about getting better at playing the piano.

"You grabbed your music books?" Mrs. Tunney asked him, smiling. "We're headed to your lesson straight after school."

"Yeah, I've got them," Broden answered, trying to speak politely to his mother.

"Good," Mrs. Tunney said, looking very happy. "I think you'll actually *enjoy* this lesson, Broden. You've put in a lot of hard work and I believe your pieces are ready to be passed off. I'm proud of you."

"Thanks, Mom," Broden said a little bashfully. Well, at least *she* was happy.

"I…uh…no offense, Broden, but I'm glad you practiced, too—I'm ready for you to practice new pieces. *Not* the A, B, C, song or…well, any of the others,"

Ellie piped up, looking away from her book and at him.

Without saying anything else, his little sister looked back at her book and started humming the tune to the song everyone hoped he would graduate from.

"Here we are," his mother sang as she pulled up to the school in the long line of cars. "I'll see you after for your lesson."

"Bye, Mom," he and Ellie called out as they shut the sliding door of the van, then hurried up to the playground to run, slide or swing until the bell rang.

All day long, he carried those heavy piano books around, feeling annoyed by them. He wished that they weren't in there and he wished he could quit.

Worse yet, when they were at recess, Jim asked if he could come over to play after school and Broden was even *more* annoyed.

"This piano stuff is taking up all of my *time*," he grumbled to himself in his mind.

"No, Jim. I can't play. I've got a lesson after school," Broden said, frowning.

"*Lesson?*" Jim asked, confused. "What kinda lesson?"

"A *piano* lesson," Broden grunted. "It's right after school."

"You take *piano lessons?*" Jim asked loudly, shocked.

Right then, Fergus walked by with his gang. Pointing and laughing, he jeered, "Har, har! The City-Sissy plays the piano!

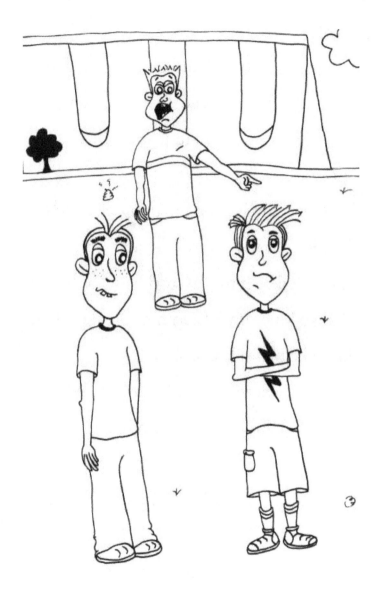

Probably cute, pretty lullabies! Har, har, har!"

"It is better than anything *you* do, Fergus," Broden said to Fergus angrily. But it was no use. He just laughed even more.

Not really having anything else to do, Broden walked away with Jim and mumbled at him, "Why'd ya have to say that so loud, Jim? *Every* mom makes their kid take piano lessons."

"Not where *we* live," Jim replied and looked at Broden as if he had ten fingers growing out of the top of his head.

"Well, my mom's making me," Broden muttered and then the bell rang and they went in for the last bit of school.

To make matters worse, Fergus kept humming famous classical music mixed in with baby songs—all of them stuff that Broden would never dream of listening to.

All of it was a nightmare that he would probably have to live through playing someday in his long, long, long, long commitment to learning to play the piano.

"*Why* doesn't Ms. Orla ever stop Fergus when he's doing terrible things like this?" Broden asked himself in despair as his pretty, red-haired teacher actually *smiled* at Fergus' humming.

Broden shook his head and wished for school to end. And to time-travel past his piano lesson.

Though he didn't get both wishes, one came true and school was soon let out. Standing up, Broden shoved everything into his backpack and rushed out of the room.

Broden couldn't believe that running out to the van that would take him to a piano lesson was better than sticking around to talk to kids about piano lessons.

5 THE PIANO LESSON

"HI HONEY! READY for your lesson?" his mother asked as soon as Broden plopped himself down into the van.

"Yup," he said, once again trying to be respectful and not adding in a plea to quit.

"Doesn't it feel so much better going to a lesson when you've prepared for it?" his mother asked, smiling at him.

"Sure, Mom," Broden said kindly, but it wasn't true. A horrible feeling was building up in his stomach as they got closer and closer to Mrs. Quinn's studio. He couldn't help but think, *I don't want to go in. I don't want to go in. I don't want to go in!*

Whether he wanted to go or not, they soon pulled up and Broden walked the long, dreadful way to the door. Much, *much* sooner than he wanted to, he was sitting on the piano bench.

Flipping open the books, his fingers were sure as he easily plunked down all of the correct keys. All of the right words came out of his mouth as he sang the tunes that had caused him so much trouble. Finally, he sighed deeply when he played through the last of his pieces.

"Oh, Broden! I just *knew* that you

could play the piano beautifully if you practiced carefully," Mrs. Quinn said. "I'm just so proud of you."

Broden looked at his teacher that had brown hair and looked a lot like his mother. He had to admit, even though he had hated practicing, it *did* feel nice to have a good lesson and get compliments from Mrs. Quinn.

"Thanks," Broden said happily.

"Well, let's continue on with your lesson! We have two things that need to be done. First, we need to take a quick look at the next pieces in the books. After that, we need to pick a special piece," Mrs. Quinn said and Broden looked at her with curiousity.

"A special piece?" he questioned.

"Yes! Today is the day that we pick out a piece for the—" Mrs. Quinn paused dramatically, then clapped her hands once as she spoke jubilantly, "recital!"

"Oh," Broden said, not really understanding what she was talking about. But then it hit him. "Wait. What? *Recital?*"

"Yes! Isn't it exciting?" Mrs. Quinn said, then stood up and went over to her bookshelf that was filled with music. "We'll pick out a piece now so that you can prepare carefully. I want you to have a *wonderful* time at the recital."

"Uhhh," Broden said, a gurgling noise coming out of his throat. "But Mrs.

46

Quinn, I don't think that I can play in a recital."

"Oh, sure you can! All of my students play and do wonderfully," she smiled and Broden suddenly found himself being gently pushed off of the bench and into his teacher's chair when she flipped open a book and began playing.

Broden thought she sounded *great*. He didn't realize that somebody could make the piano sound so brilliant.

It only took a moment before Broden relaxed while he listened. He had completely forgotten that he was supposed to be picking out a piece to play at a recital that he didn't want to perform in.

Mrs. Quinn looked at him after finishing, taking her hands off of the keys. "What do you think of that piece? Would you like to play that one for the recital?"

As soon as she turned to him, Broden remembered *exactly* what was happening and he felt like a cat that had been thrown into a pool of water. Or maybe a cat trapped in a box.

Or maybe not a cat at all, but a boy that would rather never eat cookies again in his whole entire life than play in a piano recital.

"Well…" he said, trying to figure out what to say. Pausing, a little bit of a naughty thought came to his mind—a way to get out of the recital. Maybe if he never picked a piece, he wouldn't have to play in the recital? After all, he couldn't play *Nothing* at the recital.

"Ya know, I don't really want to play that one," he said after pretending to think about the piece for a moment.

"No problem! Tell me as soon as you know if you like it or not. That way we can get through as many pieces as possible since we don't have much lesson time left," Mrs. Quinn said, smiling at him.

"Alright," Broden replied. But deep down, he knew he wouldn't say *anything* to stop her. Not only was it super fun to hear her play so many interesting pieces of music, but he was terrified of that recital. All decisions, naughty or not, would be made to get out of playing in front of a bunch of people.

Sitting back, listening and watching Mrs. Quinn's cat, Midnight, out the window, Broden listened to the great music, quite impressed with his teacher.

"What about this one?" Mrs. Quinn asked about another piece, and Broden once again pretended to consider it carefully before saying no to it, too.

For the next fifteen minutes, Mrs. Quinn played, Broden pretended to think, then he said 'not quite right,' or 'I don't think my chicken would like that one,' or 'my dad says I can't play pieces like that.'

"Broden, I can see that this piece means a lot to you. That's *wonderful*," she said, then handed him all of his books, including the book that had the recital music in it.

Yes...yes! I've won! I won't have to play! We ran out of time, Broden thought happily. He could and *would* use the same tactics *every week* until it was too late for him to learn a piece.

"So! What we'll do is have you take the book home and I'll let your mom know that she can help you pick out a piece during the week," Mrs. Quinn finished.

Heart sinking, he realized he had been *so* wrong—the trick hadn't worked. In fact, this might be *worse* than picking out a piece with Mrs. Quinn.

At least his mother wouldn't have known about the recital if he would have just picked out a piece.

Mrs. Quinn patted his shoulder and then followed him out the door to the van where his mom was waiting.

When she explained that the recital was coming and that Broden would need a piece, he felt his cheeks get red hot. Mrs. Quinn had seen right through him and his tactics.

"I'm excited to see what you choose next week," Mrs. Quinn said, then went back into the studio.

Hiding, Broden scrunched up his face in the back seat as his mother chatted happily about the recital, getting him a tie, and the fun they would have picking out a piece together. All he could do was grumpily think, "Way to go, Broden."

6 MRS. TUNNEY'S AWFUL TUNES

THE NEXT DAY after school, Broden had to practice and pick out a recital piece, but Broden had a plan. He would just have to do the same thing with his mother that he did with Mrs. Quinn.

His piano teacher had believed he was enjoying the music and simply hadn't found the right piece, so why wouldn't his mother? Although he wasn't really sure it would work, he *had* to try.

"Okay, Broden, you ready to pick out that recital piece?" his mother asked after he and Cookie had skated around the driveway for fifteen minutes.

"Yup!" he said, making himself sound excited. Although, truthfully, he kind of was. It would be nice to sit and listen to his mother play the piano, just like Mrs. Quinn. At least *he* wouldn't be playing the thing.

There was one small problem, though—his mother *didn't* play the piano 'just like Mrs. Quinn.' In fact, when she played, it hurt his ears a little bit like the blaring of a fire alarm did. The notes were all so *wrong* and *wonky* sounding.

"How do you like that one, Broden?" his mother asked as soon as she was done, and Broden came *this close* to saying he liked it fine and it would be a great piece for him to play. Wouldn't that be better than hearing more of her music?

"Well, it's a little hard to tell..." Broden said, trying to choose his words carefully so that he wouldn't hurt his mother's feelings.

It *was* hard to tell, though! It sounded more like a rhino stomping on the piano keys than his mother's fingers playing a recognizable tune.

On the other hand, the thought of the recital was terrifying. He considered the tricky situation for a moment and decided that it would be better to hear his mother play some more than to have to perform in the recital. "You know, I think I'd better hear another one to *really* be able to choose."

He felt dizzy as she played wrong notes galore during the second piece, asking him once more, "How do you like that one, Broden?"

"Uh…well…I guess it was pretty good, but I think I just want to hear all of the pieces before I choose," Broden said, trying to hide his relief that her super awful playing was finally over.

"That's a good idea. I can do that," Mrs. Tunney said happily. She flipped the page and the rest of the musical torture began.

There were moments when Broden wanted to cry out for her to stop, but the longer he sat, the more he realized that he *could not* play in the piano recital. He might sound like *his mom!* It made him even more determined to not pick a piece.

"That's the last of the pieces, Broden! Which one do you like the best?" his mother asked when the horrifying sounds finally stopped.

Broden stared at his mother—he couldn't believe that she had played every single piece. And he couldn't believe how *bad* she was at playing. Maybe *she* was the one that ought to be taking piano lessons.

"Broden?" his mother asked again, this time not so cheerily. She didn't really like it when he stared.

"Uh, Mom, I'm not really sure..." he said, trying to figure out what to say. "Maybe you can play them one more time?"

"No, Broden. You heard all of them yesterday, now you've heard them all again," Mrs. Tunney said.

Broden had to keep himself from saying that she hadn't *really* played them for him and that he couldn't even tell what most of them *were*.

"It's time to pick," his mom said, looking at him expectantly.

"But I don't know what to pick," Broden said, panicking that his mother wouldn't play anything else for him.

"Broden, you've heard them all twice

now. You've got to have *some* idea of what you would like to choose," Mrs. Tunney persisted.

"Not really, Mom," Broden said, getting upset. "I really think it would help if you would play them for me once more."

"Broden, I'm not going to play *all* of them for you again. I'll play two or three, but that's it, son," Mrs. Tunney said, her voice becoming stern.

"Okay," Broden pouted, glad she'd play some more, though his ears weren't happy about it.

Then came the questions about which piece he liked best. Lots of questions all coming so fast that Broden couldn't think or answer quickly enough before his mother asked yet another one.

It was especially difficult because he was so upset about the recital. He couldn't stand the thought of performing in it.

"Did you like this one? This one was lovely, but do you want to play a slow piece or would you prefer something faster? Would you like to play a piece that sounds happy or sad? Fast or slow? Short or long?" she asked and finally Broden couldn't take it any more.

"I don't want to play *any of them!*" Broden cried out, grabbing his hair. "I can't perform in a *recital*. It's terrifying!"

Mrs. Tunney stopped talking and

snapped her mouth shut. She looked at him for a *long* time. Then she blinked twice.

"Oh, honey. Don't worry about playing in the recital. It'll be wonderful," his mother said, her voice returning to the lovely one she usually used.

"But there will be so many *people*, and what if I mess up?" Broden asked anxiously. He left out the part where he wanted to say, 'What if I sound like *you?*'

Standing up, his mother pushed the bench in and Broden hoped she wouldn't leave before saying something that would make him feel better.

"Sweetheart, I promise that there will be at least one good thing that happens from the recital," she responded, smiling. "Maybe it won't be that you play *perfectly,* and maybe you won't enjoy it. But I promise that it will be good for your character to try something new."

Broden didn't *like* it when his parents spoke about something being good for his *character.* That usually just meant that it was something that he *had* to do that would be really, really hard. And he probably wouldn't like it.

"Maybe the only good thing will be the ice cream sundaes at home to celebrate," his mother said in her sing-song voice. "Your father and I want you to perform in this recital. But…if it's really so terrible for you, we'll let you skip the next one

before doing another."

Looking at his smiling, soft, pretty mother that offered some sympathy—and a reward—he felt a little better.

"That sounds pretty good. Shake on it?" Broden stuck out his hand and his mother took it to seal the deal. Then she pulled him in to a hug.

Taking a deep breath, he caught the scent of his mother—warm clothes, fresh-baked muffins, and comfort.

"Broden, I want to get started on dinner so that you, Dad and Ellie don't turn into a ravenous pack of wolves. Why don't you take your book upstairs to think about what you want to play?" Mrs. Tunney handed him the book and gently guided him toward the stairs. "After dinner, I'll help you finish picking, okay?"

"Okay," Broden said, then raced up the stairs. Somehow, now it didn't seem so bad.

7 COOKIE WISDOM

LAYING ON THE BED, Broden flipped through the music book, trying to remember the way Mrs. Quinn played the pieces—*not* the way his mother had.

Broden looked and looked and *looked,* but, except for tabbing the pages of the fast pieces, he didn't know which one to choose.

Scratch, scratch, came a sound that Broden knew so well. Looking over at the tiny door in his room that led out to the attic, Broden saw his cute, little

Cookie-chicken peck the door open and come *buk-buk-buk-buking* over to the bed. One hop and she landed on his bed right next to him.

"Hiya Cookie," Broden said and patted his chicken's back. She took it as an invitation and climbed right up on top of his tummy, then nested on him like he was a giant egg that she was keeping warm.

"Cookie!" Broden pretended to scold. "I'm supposed to be picking out some music! How am I supposed to do that if you're *sitting* on me?"

"Buk-buk-buk," she said, which he had learned meant, 'I don't know,' in chicken. Then she looked around the room and let out little purring, humming noises that she only made when she was happy.

Holding the book up in the air above Cookie, Broden looked at the music once more, shaking his head. "Cookie, I have to play in a piano recital. Which piece should I choose? I just don't know how to pick!"

"Buk-buk?" Cookie became alert and looked at him, cocking her head.

"Yes, *really*," Broden answered.

With that, Cookie got up and began busily clucking and scratching through his things that were on the ground in his room.

Using her beak, she picked up a book, moved a kite and finally hopped her big chicken bum into a box of army men. Scratching and pecking through each figure, she finally knocked it over as she got out.

"Cookie, stop making a mess of my toys," Broden said sternly, but then he apologized when she gave him the evil eye. "Sorry, Cook."

"Bok-bok-bok," she said, accepting his apology.

Next, the little chicken clucked over to a pile of dirty clothes. She picked up a shirt, another shirt, then a pair of pants. When she picked up a dirty sock, she scrunched up her beak and spit it out, clicking her beak and grunting in disgust.

Broden laughed, but after that, she

picked up a pair of his undies just as he cried out, "Not those, Cookie!"

Cookie's eyes popped open wide, she opened up her cookie-cutter-shark-toothed mouth and *screeched*.

Flapping wildly, she ran all around the room, yelling, *"Booooooooooook-kuk-kuk-buuuuuk-a-bok!"*

"Sorry, Cookie! Sorry!" Broden cried, but he couldn't help but laugh a bit.

However, now Cookie was grumpy. She scratched harder at the toys and she didn't really pick anything else up with her mouth. And she kept muttering, *"Cluck, cluck, cluck…"*

Broden sat up, opened the music book to a piece that he liked pretty well and lay it in front of him on the bed. Looking at all of the black notes and musical symbols on the white page, it looked kind of hard, but not too terrible. He said, "The name is pretty cool...*Zebra Stampede...*"

Suddenly, something went *PLOP!* into his lap and, looking down, Broden saw that Cookie had dropped Eagle Man onto his legs.

"Thanks, Cookie," Broden said. He picked up the action figure, then kept looking at the music that was laying on the bed in front of him.

"Buk, buk," Cookie said. Then she did something crazy. She swung one little chicken leg back, then *swooshed* it forward with all of her might. Her claw *crashed* into the music book and kicked it *right off of the bed.*

"Cookie! That's my book," Broden exclaimed. Hopping off the bed, he grabbed the piano book from the floor, sending Eagle Man tumbling to the ground as he did so.

Turning through the pages once more, Broden was surprised when, once again, Cookie dumped Eagle Man into his lap, then plopped herself onto his music.

When Broden tried to nudge her off, Cookie showed her shark teeth and said, "Buk-buk."

Broden was shocked! Cookie *never* told him to 'stop it.'

Cookie nudged Eagle Man toward him with her beak and looked at him with a wise expression.

Broden looked deeply into her eyes, but he just didn't understand. "What are you trying to tell me, Cookie?"

The little hen, with her majestically beautiful black feathers that shimmered blue and purple, stood up on his music.

Stretching up her neck, Cookie looked at him proudly. Then, she opened her mouth.

What happened next was incredible. With her lovely beak open, Cookie began…to sing. A song without any words, only sweet notes slipping along.

Every, single note came out perfectly and the sound rang around Broden's room. It was as if he could almost *see* the beautiful sound that spun a magical tune through the air.

So enchanted was Broden with Cookie's song, she was halfway through the clear melody before he even realized that he *knew* her song without words. Only, with Cookie singing, it was much more beautiful than any human ever would have been able to make it.

"Eagle Man Soar. Eagle Man Fly," Broden began to sing as gently as Cookie was. *"Eagle Man will see you with his awesome eye. Bad guys, run away as fast as you can—if you don't you'll get caught by an eagle that's half*

man. *Eagle Man, Eagle Man, Eagle, Eagle Maaaan.*"

Cookie hopped into his lap when their duet was finished. She looked at him and smiled. "Buk *bok* buk."

"Play *that* song, huh?" Broden looked at his chicken and stroked her feathers. "Cookie, that was the most beautiful singing I've ever heard. And that's the best idea in the world. Thank you."

"Buk-buk-buk," she said and Broden understood that her chicken words meant, 'You're welcome.'

"I'm gonna go and see if Mom will get that music for me," Broden said excitedly. "Is that ok with you?"

"Buk-a-buk-a-buk," Cookie replied,

flapped off of the bed, then went back out the attic door.

Flinging his legs over the side of the bed, Broden hopped off and ran out of his bedroom, zooming downstairs to his mother. "Mom! Mom, Cookie—I mean, I had an idea!"

Broden found his mother in the kitchen with all sorts of good smells coming from the pans where she worked her spells. Looking up from stirring she asked, "What kind of idea did you have?"

"Can I play Eagle Man for the recital? I really, *really* want to!" Broden exclaimed and looked at his mother expectantly.

"Wow, Broden," Mrs. Tunney replied, surprised. She bit her lip and thought for a moment, then, "It might be a little tricky, but I think we can make that work. What a great idea, son. I'm glad you found something that you love."

"Thanks, Mom," Broden said happily, then snagged a slice of chopped carrot.

"Let's get over to the music shop right after dinner. Okay, little thief?" she spoke teasingly, then pinched his cheek.

"Yeah! Sounds great!" Broden called back to her as he ran away from her cheek-pinching.

8 GREASY HAIR

AFTER DINNER, Broden and his mother went together on a special drive to the music store, *Instruments, Music & More!* Broden thought that it smelled like wood, old paper, dust and greasy hair. Looking at the man working behind the counter, he understood at least *one* of the smells.

"Hello, there. My son here loves the cartoon, *Eagle Man: Hero of the World.* He has an upcoming piano recital and wants to play the theme song. We came to see

if you might have the music for it," his mother said sweetly and the man happily showed her where she might find that sort of music.

"My grandson loves that Eagle Man, too. I've watched maybe an episode or two with him. Not bad at all," he said, and Broden thought that maybe it didn't smell too much like greasy hair in the shop.

"You know, the sheet music could be here in this stack," the man said to Broden when they couldn't find it on the shelves, holding out a pile of piano solos. "Go on and dig through it."

"Thank you, sir," Broden responded and began digging while his mother kept searching through bins, and on the shelves.

"No…no…that's not it…hmmm…" Broden said as he read through each piece of music.

Feeling a little gloomy when he only had one piece of music left to check, he crossed his toes, then flipped it over to check the final title.

Reading the words, he gasped, then whispered, *"Eagle Man; Hero of the World Theme Song."*

"Yes!" he cried, then rushed over to his mother. "I found it! I found it, Mom!"

"Broden, I'm so glad. I wasn't sure if they'd have it," she happily replied. "Let's take a look at it to make sure it's your level."

Mrs. Tunney flipped open the music and furrowed her brow. Then she went and took it to one of the pianos in the shop and plunked some of the notes out. "Well, it's a little trickier than those other pieces…"

"It's ok, Mom. I promise!" Broden said, thrilled that he might be able to play the Eagle Man theme song for *real*, even if it was a little hard. "I know I can do it."

"If you feel like this is what you want, then we'll get it," she replied. "I'm proud of you, son. This will be great."

"Thanks for getting it, Mom," Broden said and then he followed his mother to the payment counter.

He looked at the music all the way home, playing the notes on imaginary keys on his lap as they drove along in the van.

"I'm gonna go practice right now!" Broden called out as soon as the van parked and he hopped out of the van. Rushing inside and straight to the piano, he began plunking away.

9 TEACHER COOKIE

BRODEN HAD FUN PLAYING the Eagle Man theme song all week long. It was the most wonderful thing that he had ever played.

The only problem was that it wasn't really sounding much more like Eagle Man than when he had first started practicing it.

"Mom, maybe Eagle Man really *is* too hard," Broden said the day before his piano lesson as they drove home from school. "It just doesn't seem like it sounds like it's supposed to."

"No, I don't think it's too hard," Mrs. Tunney replied. "But, as happy as I am that you're playing it, you need to practice more slowly. And count. And you especially need to check your notes. You make a lot of note mistakes."

"No, I don't," Broden mumbled, feeling a little defensive at his mother's hen-pecking critique. "It's too hard!"

"Listen, sweetheart. You've only had it a few days. Let Mrs. Quinn help you with it tomorrow and make sure you do your best today, okay?" his mother said as she smiled at him in the mirror.

"Alrighty," Broden responded. Then he hummed the theme song all the way home until they were parked in the garage.

"Fifteen minutes, then head inside," his mother called as he grabbed his skateboard. "Oh! And while you do your piano work, I'm taking Ellie down the road to the neighbor's for some play time. You'll have to practice on your own today."

"Okay!" Broden called and hopped onto the board.

He moved up and down the drive, worked on a new trick, and got a little stinky and sweaty.

To his disappointment, it seemed like only one minute had passed when his mother called him to the piano.

"Coming!" Broden yelled and did one last trick before putting his board away.

"Bye, Broden!" Ellie called as she came outside, followed by their mother.

"Bye, Ell," he returned. Then he got kissed on the head by his mother.

"You head inside and practice now, okay? I need to hear your pieces when I come back. And I'll know if you need to practice them more," Mrs. Tunney said with a warning voice, pointing her finger sternly at him.

"I'll do a good job. I promise," Broden replied, trying to convince her.

The only problem was, he realized how much fun it would be to skate instead of sit at the piano and a split second later, he wasn't really sure if he would practice while she was gone. Or at least, not right away.

When his mother was quite far down the street, Broden's feet began taking him toward the garage and his skateboard. Cross-his-heart, it wasn't *his* fault that his feet were being naughty.

But then that terrible, guilty, nagging feeling seemed to squish his heart like a ball of clay and *that* moved his feet in a new direction to the piano.

He sat down at the bench, whipped open Eagle Man, and began pushing down the keys. He played it quickly a few times, then stopped and stared at the music. "It just doesn't sound that much like Eagle Man."

Broden huffed as he remembered the advice his mother had given. Deep down, he knew that going slower and checking his notes would be the best thing for him…and *Eagle Man*. But that sounded like work, and a *lot* of it.

"Oh, well," Broden said, then flopped his fingers back down and began banging out Eagle Man just as he had been for several days.

Only *this* time, somebody interrupted him. "B-*wok!* B-*wok!* B-*wooook!*"

Shaking her chicken head, Cookie stomped into the room, up to the piano, and flapped once to get onto the bench.

"Aww, Cookie! You like my music?"

Broden cooed, patting his chicken's neck.

Cookie rolled her eyes, then gently pecked and pecked and pecked at Broden until he scrambled off of the bench. "Cookie, what's *that* all about?"

Broden was hurt. Or at least, his feelings were. Why was she behaving this way? As Cookie settled on the bench, though, muttering and grumbling to herself, Broden thought that he must have mistaken her words.

Cookie wasn't saying, 'Song! Song! Soooong!" The correct translation was, 'Wrong! Wrong! Wroooong!'

Settling her chicken bootie on the piano bench, then looking at him the

whole time, Cookie slowly and carefully pecked out each and every note of Eagle Man. She didn't miss a single beat, rest or note.

Then she hopped up on the keys with a *wer-ONK,* and said, "Buk-a-buk."

And that was when Cookie began to do something that Broden had *never* seen before.

With her claws and talons, she played the deep chords of Eagle Man's theme. Then, while still holding onto the chords with her feet, she began playing the awesome melody of Eagle Man with her beak. Only this time, she played *quickly.*

She was hopping and pecking all over the keyboard of the large piano, her head bobbing up and down much more rapidly than Broden had ever thought that any chicken could move. *Chord!* went the claws, then *peck, peck, peck!* went the notes of the melody.

Cookie moved wildly, focusing on her musical artistry, not even paying attention to Broden as he watched with his mouth *wide* open.

He watched, stunned, until she finally struck the last few notes and was done.

Broden stared, shocked at the chicken's performance.

"Cookie, you're amazing! I...I can't believe it. How'd you learn to do that?" Broden finally asked, and Cookie plopped herself back onto the bench and carefully…slowly…deliberately…played each note painfully sluggishly.

Cookie was telling him just what his mother had said. He needed to be more cautious and do things correctly.

Broden sighed deeply, accepting the nightmare of a truth. "Alright, Cookie. Go ahead and scoot over. I want to be like you, so I need to practice, now. And *carefully*."

The little hen hopped down and clucked her way back out the sliding door, Broden calling out a 'thank you' as she left.

All alone, Broden sat down on the bench, a little overwhelmed at the mountain of work that lay ahead of him.

But then he lifted his fingers and he practiced just the way his Cookie-Teacher had taught him. *Very slowly* and every note, rhythm and fingering done correctly.

10 BRAVO! BRAVO!

AFTER WEEKS and weeks of practicing Eagle Man's theme song *carefully*, Broden found himself sitting in a row of piano students, listening to Mrs. Quinn welcome everyone to the recital.

"I'm so glad that you all could be here today," she said brightly in front of the crowd of people.

Broden gulped again. It felt like he had a dirty sock stuck in his throat that wouldn't swallow down. Even though he had gotten more and more used to the idea, it still terrified him that he was actually sitting there, getting ready to play his piece.

"This is an exciting time of year!" she continued. "These students have worked hard on their pieces and it is wonderful that you are here to support them."

I'd rather be alone! Broden thought, feeling it would be very nice if the room were magically empty.

"Please only whisper if necessary, turn off all electronics, wait for applause before you leave or enter the recital hall, and no flash cameras. All of these things are terribly distracting to our performers, and we want them to have their best chance at their best performance."

Broden turned around and spied his mother looking at him. She gave him a thumbs up and he turned back around, trying to swallow that stinky-sock-in-the-throat feeling again.

"On that note, let's begin with Chelsea!" Mrs. Quinn announced and began clapping her hands as a little girl walked up to the front and took a bow.

Broden liked her song, but he found it incredibly difficult to sit still as he waited for his turn. Looking down the row of students, he counted in his head how many more would perform before it was his turn. *One, two, three, four.*

Now Broden didn't feel like his throat was clogged. He felt like his dinner might come up as his stomach soured at the thought that there were only four—nope! now three—more students to play before his turn.

Up and down the students went, and so quickly that Broden hardly had a moment to think about it. When the kid next to him, the last one before his turn, went up, his eyebrows began to sweat and his toes turned into ice cubes.

The boy played a piece that Broden didn't even hear a note of, and then came down after taking another bow.

Suddenly, Broden wished that he were superglued to his seat. Although, having learned how tricky Mrs. Quinn could be about getting him to accomplish things, she would probably just cheerfully lift him to the piano where he could play trapped on the seat.

There were about five seconds of silence in the big room as Broden worked up the courage to stand up. It was strange to have *so many people* waiting for him to stand.

Taking a deep breath, Broden sighed, then *creeeeeak* went his chair as he slowly rose.

Everyone began to clap for him as he walked ever so slowly up to the piano where he took a bow. He sat down and was suddenly so terrified, he wasn't certain if he actually *could* begin his performance.

But then he remembered Cookie wildly dancing on the keys and he couldn't help but think, *Cookie taught me, so I can do it…*

He put his hands on the keys. He took a breath, and then…

BOOM went the first chord in the left hand, followed by his right hand masterfully flashing like lightning along the tops of the notes.

Broden's hands swirled along together, weaving the incredible *Eagle Man* melody *even better* than he had ever played it before.

His hands bobbed up and down, *almost* the way Cookie's head did when she played on the piano. *Womp* went his left

hand chords while his right hand danced along the famous tune like a swordsman.

With his brow furrowed, Broden concentrated on creating an invisible piece of art that bounced colorfully around the room with the music's bright tones and sounds.

As he did so, Broden felt something without even noticing it; a satisfaction that he was doing something very difficult—and doing it well, even.

Finally, his practiced hands came down with a bang and the last notes resonated perfectly in the room.

Broden lifted his fingers off of the keys and he couldn't believe that he was done. It had gone so quickly once he started!

Then, wild applause broke out and Broden stood up to take a bow, smiling.

When Broden sat down, the kid next to him leaned over and said, "That was *great*. I love Eagle Man!"

At that moment, Broden realized that he actually, truly enjoyed performing, and he wouldn't make a stink about it again.

The rest of the recital went quickly, except for the taking of pictures—which he really couldn't stand—and then Mrs. Quinn came up to him, saying, "Broden, that was *wonderful*. I'm so proud of you."

Then, before he knew it, Broden found himself at home with a bowl of ice cream that had sprinkles and candy on top.

He couldn't believe how hard he had to work to play *Eagle Man* well, and he couldn't believe how quickly the recital was done.

It was strange to him that his music was something so real, and yet, it completely disappeared as soon as he lifted his fingers.

Unless you were sitting in the room while the piano was being played, you would never know that such an amazing piece of art had ever existed there. Broden decided that it was rather magical.

"I'm so proud of you, son. You worked so hard and you performed just beautifully," his mother said, patting his arm. "You did it!"

"Yeah, I did," Broden said happily. "Thanks, Mom."

After his bowl of ice cream disappeared, it was time for bed. Broden didn't mind, though. He was exhausted from the excitement of performing.

After brushing his teeth and getting tucked in, he lay in the room with star and moonlight shining in through the window.

Scratch, scratch, scratch. Broden smiled. He knew it was Cookie and that she would soon hop up and make a little nest out of his blankets next to him.

"Hiya, Cookie," Broden whispered when she hopped up with a few little clucking sounds.

"Buk-a-buk-buk," Cookie answered, using her claws and beak to make a perfect little circle for her nest.

"I did it, Cookie. I performed my best!" Broden told Cookie as he stroked under her chin.

Cookie made a little cooing sound of happiness, showing her shark-toothed smile and Broden couldn't help but return a not-so-shark-toothed smile back at his sweet little chicken.

"Thank you for helping me, Cookie," Broden said in human.

"Buk buk-buk," Cookie said in chicken.

BUK BUK
(Or in Human, 'The End')

WANT TO FIND OUT WHEN A NEW BRODEN AND COOKIE COMES OUT?

Sign up for the Readers' List at

www.katiecoughran.com/broden-and-cookie-free-coloring-pages-with-readers-list-sign-up

Enter the link to grab free coloring pages, books and find out about Broden and Cookie happenings!

There are more Broden and Cookie books! Find a full list at KatieCoughran.com, or you can search wherever books are sold online for these titles:

Broden and the Shark-Toothed Chicken

Broden and the Jellybean

Broden Wants to Quit

If you like the Broden and Cookie books and want to read more of their adventures, please help by leaving a review on Amazon.com. Buk-Buk for your support! Or in human, Thank You!

116

ABOUT THE AUTHOR

Katie Coughran is the independent author and illustrator of the Broden and Cookie chapter book series. She also writes young adult fantasy and fiction. You can find out more about all of her other books on KatieCoughran.com.

Katie lives in the Pacific Northwest with her handsome husband and two delightful children where they love to walk, camp and enjoy meals outside. They live with their menagerie of animals; four chickens (yes, one is named Cookie), Sneaky the cat, and Oliver the wiener dog.

CPSIA information can be obtained
at www.ICGtesting.com
Printed in the USA
BVHW030240021220
594670BV00025B/221